A Gift from
Winklesea

Other books by Helen Cresswell

Whatever Happened in Winklesea?
Mystery at Winklesea
A Game of Catch
The Little Sea Horse

A Gift from **Winklesea**

Helen Cresswell

Illustrated by Susan Winter

a division of Hodder Headline

First published by Brockhampton Press 1969

This edition first published 1995
by Hodder Children's Books

10 9 8 7 6 5 4 3 2

A Catalogue record for this book is available from the British Library

ISBN 0 340 71501 4

Typeset by Phoenix Typesetting, Ilkley, West Yorkshire

Printed and bound in Great Britain by
Clays Ltd, St Ives plc

Hodder Children's Books
a division of Hodder Headline plc
338 Euston Road
London NW1 3BH

Contents

One

The Outing

The day before the Children's Outing to Winklesea Dan and Mary opened their money-boxes.

"There might be pounds!" cried Mary, shaking hers. It was an enormous pig, white with blue spots. It wore a smile so contented that it looked as if it really *might* have swallowed a fortune.

"We've been saving long enough," Dan said. "Let's feel whose is heaviest."

His was a pillar-box that locked properly. He had given the key to their mother for safe keeping weeks ago, after he had been tempted to take out some money for sweets.

"Mine's heaviest!" cried Mary.

"Only because it's full of pennies," Dan said.

Mary changed most of her money into pennies. She then had a satisfying pile to be pushed through the slot on the pig's back. Lately, though, she had had to change to fivepences. The pig was full – or nearly.

Their mother came in with Dan's key.

"Here we are. Now let's see what we've got."

Dan unlocked his door and a silver stream slid on to the table. He whistled between his teeth and a slow grin spread over his face.

"Look at *that*!" he said. Then he began counting.

"Open mine!" cried Mary. Her pig

had a large cork underneath. It was too stiff for her to move. She had tried it.

Mrs Kane eased the cork slowly round. All at once it came out and a rattling shower of copper poured from the hole. Dan glanced from his counting.

"I told you," he said. "Pennies."

Mary lifted the pig and began to shake. Pennies, pennies, pennies. The pile grew to a little mountain. Then, like snow on its cap, came the silver fivepences, and even the magic glint of a tenpenny piece.

"There *is* pounds!" she cried. "Pounds and pounds!"

Half an hour later everything was reckoned up. Dan had two pounds sixteen. Mary had one pound eight and three buttons.

"And it's far too much," said their mother. "One pound each, and that's plenty."

"Oh, Mum!" cried Dan. "What about the roundabouts and things?"

"And buckets and spades and flags for sandcastles," said Mary, "and ice-cream and windmills and sweets and beachballs!"

"A pound each," repeated their mother. "That's plenty. Both of you put one pound into a pile, and I'll change it into tenpenny pieces. That's the best way to take it, in silver."

"What about the rest?" Mary asked.

"Put it back in the pig, of course," she said. "Start saving for something else."

"My birthday," suggested Dan. "Only six weeks now. Everyone get saving."

So the two Kanes set off on the outing with a pound each to spend.

"And listen," Dan said to Mary as the bus turned out from the car park and all the children turned to wave to their parents. "*Save* some, see? We've both got to save some."

"For a present, you mean?" Mary asked.

Dan nodded.

"We'll get Mum something really good if we both club together."

"Some hankies," suggested Mary. "Or a necklace. She'd like that."

"You don't bring *hankies* back from the seaside," Dan said. "You can get those anywhere. You bring something special. A real *seaside* thing. You know – made of shells or something."

"Oh yes! You can even get little ladies made of shells."

"I don't know about that," Dan said. "But something *like* that."

Then someone at the back started singing and everyone joined in. And then at last they were at Winklesea itself with its pier and funfair and miles of shell-strewn sands. They paddled, made castles, rode on roundabouts and ate endless bags of potato crisps.

Half an hour before the bus left for home Mary and Dan remembered the present.

"I know where to get it," Dan said. "There's a shop on the front."

"Where I got my bucket and spade," said Mary. "They had some shell ladies. I saw them."

"How much have we got, first?" said Dan. "Hand yours over and I'll count it up."

Mary dug her purse from her bag and Dan emptied his pockets.

"Forty-six pence," said Dan. "Come on, let's see what there is."

"There!" cried Mary as they peered into the window. "Forty pence! We can get it!"

She pointed at the cockleshell lady perched on a shiny base that said "A Gift from Winklesea".

"I don't think Mum would like it," Dan said. He certainly did not. "What about that?"

He pointed.

"What?" said Mary. She had steamed up her patch of window and edged along to get a better view.

"That corkscrew and tin-opener. Thirty-five pence."

"But that's not a proper *seaside* present," Mary said. "It's not made of shells. And it doesn't even say it's from Winklesea. Ooh Dan! Look! What about that?"

"Now what?"

"That egg! That beautiful egg!"

They stared at it together. It was an

egg-shaped stone, bluish green, mounted on a pedestal of cockles. On it, in beautiful gold letters was "A Gift from Winklesea". It was perfect. They both knew it.

"What *is* it?" said Dan.

"It can go on the mantelpiece!" cried Mary.

"Forty pence," Dan said. "That'll be enough left over for a bag of crisps each. Come on."

They went in, ducking under festoons of rubber rings and rope sandals. The lady behind the counter took the stone egg from the window.

"What is it, please?" Mary asked.

The lady shrugged.

"Ornament," she said. "Could use it as a paper-weight, I suppose. Pretty stone, though. Found it myself, as a matter of fact, a couple of weeks back. Thought it was an egg, I did, when I saw it lying there."

"It's definitely *not* an egg, is it?" Dan said. "I mean, it won't break?"

She laughed and rapped on the stone with her pen.

"Stone all right," she said. "Weighs heavy, as well. Want it in a box with cotton-wool? Present, is it?"

Dan nodded.

"Five pence extra," she said, taking out a silver cardboard box and packing it with cotton wool.

"There go the crisps!" said Dan under his breath.

Mary did not mind. She took the silver box and put it in her bag. On the way home she kept taking it out and opening it and looking at the greenish stone with "A Gift from Winklesea" in that beautiful gold lettering. It can go on the mantelpiece between the clock and the green glass cat, she decided. Then she fell asleep.

Two

Stone – or Egg?

The stone egg did go on the mantelpiece between the clock and the green glass cat. It was too beautiful to go anywhere else. Even their father liked it – you could tell that by the jokes he made about it.

"Funny hen that laid *that* egg," he said when he first saw it. "All that gold lettering. I've heard of hens that lay eggs with lions on – but gold letters! That *is* something!"

Uncle Fred had been there at the time.

"Mind it don't hatch out," he said. "It's a bit warmish there over that gas fire."

"The chicken that comes out of that egg'd have to have a sharp beak," said Mr Kane. He rapped hard on the polished stone.

"Well I think it's lovely," said Mrs Kane. "They couldn't have picked anything I'd have liked better."

Dan and Mary exchanged smug looks, the subject was changed, and in a few days the Gift from Winklesea had become part of the furniture. People always noticed it when they came into the room though, and Mary would go and take it carefully down to show it off.

About two weeks later one of their mother's friends had been admiring it. After she had gone, Mary said, "Listen,

Dan, there's something funny about that stone."

"What?" asked Dan. He was making a model aeroplane and only half listening.

"Whenever I get hold of it," said Mary, "it feels warm."

"What of it?" Dan's head was still bent. "It's over the fireplace, isn't it?"

"Yes, but Dan, the fire isn't *on*."

Now he did lift his head.

"Bring it here," he commanded.

Mary reached up and carefully lifted it down. She cupped her hand over the smooth sides of the stone as she always did, and again felt that faint warmth. Once she had stayed on a farm and helped lift the hens' eggs from the nesting boxes. It felt like those had done. Now Dan, too, placed his hand over the greenish stone.

"Mmmmm." He hardly liked to admit that it *was* warm. Why on earth should it be?

"Warmish, I suppose. Only a bit,

though. It isn't exactly freezing today, you know."

"Yes, but it's stone," said Mary. "And stones are usually cold."

They stared at each other.

"You don't think – you don't think that it *will* hatch out, do you?" she said.

Dan burst out laughing.

"Hatch out!" he cried. "Honestly, Mary! A *stone*? It's just a big pebble, that's all. What do you think's going to hatch out of that? A chicken?"

"I don't know," admitted Mary. "Nothing really, I suppose. I know it's really only a stone."

"I'll tell you what," Dan said, "we'll do an experiment."

He was keen on experiments. His last one had been a complicated one to do with measuring rainfall. This one would be simple.

"What we'll do," he said, "is get a stone out of the garden. Just a nice, big, ordinary stone. Then we'll put it on the mantelpiece next to the other one. Right?"

"Right," said Mary. She often helped with Dan's experiments. She never understood them, but she helped anyway.

"Then," said Dan, "tomorrow we'll feel them both together. Test them. See if one of them's warmer than the other."

"Yes!" she cried. "I see!" She really did see, for once. Usually she just pretended that she did. "I'll go and find a stone straight away."

"Make sure it's about the same size," Dan called after her.

She went out into the small garden behind the house. At the bottom was a wicket gate leading on to the tow path that ran along the edge of the canal. That would be the best place for finding a stone, but she was not allowed through the gate alone, so she began to search the flower beds. At last she found the very thing, among the cabbages. It felt cold and heavy in her hand, and the faintest of shivers ran down her back.

"It's *ten* times colder than the other one," she thought.

She told Dan so when she went back inside.

"Of course it is," he said. "It's been outside in the soil, hasn't it? Better give it a wash before you put it on the shelf, or you'll have Mum after you."

"*Us*," said Mary. "Not just me. It was your idea."

She gave the stone a good wash in soapy water, dried it on the tea towel and put it on the mantelpiece right next to the Gift from Winklesea.

"It looks quite nice," she said. "Probably all stones would, if they had a good wash and polish."

"I shouldn't think Mum will think so," Dan said.

"How long will we have to wait?" she asked. She watched the two stones as if she expected something to happen there and then, right under her very eyes.

"Till tomorrow." Dan had lost interest again. He had just reached a tricky bit of glueing and Mary knew it was no use trying to talk to him.

She felt restless and fidgety. She tried to do a jigsaw. Every now and then she got up and felt the two stones. After about the sixth time she said, "It *is* warm. The one out of the garden, I mean. I'm sure it's getting warmer."

"Of course it is! Getting up every five minutes and picking it up. It's getting the warmth out of your hands. Leave it alone. Forget it."

Mary left it alone, but she did not forget it. The evening seemed endless and next morning when she awoke she remembered in the very instant of opening her eyes. She went into Dan's room where he was sitting up in bed reading.

"Come on!" she whispered. Their parents were still asleep.

He stared at her.

"Come on where?" he demanded.

"Downstairs. To feel the eggs. The experiment."

"Oh *that*!"

"Dan, come on. *Please*!"

"Oh, all right."

He swung his legs out of bed.

Downstairs in the dim sitting-room,

the curtains still closed from the night before, they tiptoed to the mantelpiece. It felt rather like Christmas. Carefully Dan placed his hands over the two stones. Mary watched his face. For a few moments he said nothing. Then a look of amazement spread over his face.

"It *is* warm!" he said. He took his hands away suddenly.

Mary touched first the cool, hard surface of the garden stone then, gingerly, the Gift from Winklesea. There it was again – that strange, almost *living* warmth.

The two of them stared at each other in the dim light. The clock ticked loudly right by their ear.

"It *is* going to hatch out," said Mary at last in a whisper.

Dan nodded slowly.

"Looks like it. But what into? That's the point – what *into*?"

Three

Hatched

As it happened, the Kanes were just sitting down to a fish and chip supper when the egg started to hatch out.

"Nice bit of plaice, this," said Mr Kane. "Switch that blessed row off, for a minute, will you? Can't hear myself eat."

Mary got down and went to the television. She waited till the lady had finished telling everyone to use the same soap as she did, then turned off. It always seemed rather rude to switch off when people were right in the middle of a sentence.

"That's better," said Mr Kane. "Thanks. Tomato sauce?"

Mary began to decorate her chips with little scarlet splashes. Then she too picked up her knife and fork and began. No one spoke.

It was then that Mary heard the noise. Tap, tap, tap! She looked up. Everyone else was busy eating.

"Tap, tap, tap!" It was louder this time.

"What's that?" said Mrs Kane, listening. They all listened. It came again.

"Where's it coming from?" said Dan, looking round.

At that moment Mary let out a squeal. "Look! Look!"

She pointed dumbly to the mantlepiece. There, beside the prim green glass cat, was the Gift from Winklesea rocking, absolutely *rocking* on its cockleshell pedestal. Mrs Kane squealed too. All four of them got up and advanced slowly towards the fireplace. The tapping was louder now, and continuous. The greenish stone jumped and quivered.

"It's – it's come unglued," said Mrs Kane faintly at last.

"I should just think it has," said Mr Kane. "Jumping about like that! Whatever's got into it?"

That was the question. What *had* got into it?

"It's going to hatch," Dan said. "Any minute, I should think."

"Hatch!" Mrs Kane fairly screamed. "Hatch?"

"Looks like it, Mother," said Mr Kane cautiously. "There's *something* banging away in there, that's certain."

Mrs Kane sat down suddenly. She just sat there, staring up at the Gift from Winklesea doing its strange, solitary dance up there on its cockleshell pedestal.

"*Do* something," she said at last. "You and your jokes about it hatching out!"

Mr Kane cleared his throat.

"Could *be* some kind of joke, I suppose," he said. "It didn't say anything on it about it's being a joke, did it?"

Dan and Mary shook their heads silently without moving their eyes from the jogging stone.

"The chips are getting cold," moaned Mrs Kane. "Oh dear, what a thing to happen!"

"Well then," said Mr Kane loudly, as if hoping that the egg would hear him, "we'll get *on* with our chips. We can't stand round all night looking at this thing showing off. Come alone, Dan, come on, Mary, get on with your suppers. Take no notice of it."

They went slowly back to the table. They picked up their knives and forks again. All the while, louder and louder, came that tap, tapping as the egg jumped and jogged.

"Looks like being a nice day again to-morrow," said Mr Kane loudly. "Though we could do with a drop of rain, for the lettuce and tomatoes."

Tap, tap, tap, tap.

"The sweet peas look like doing nicely

this year," almost shouted Mr Kane.

At that moment the egg, with a final acrobatic leap, jumped right clear of the pedestal and landed smack at the feet of the glass cat. Mary and Mrs Kane screamed together. Then, knives and forks poised in mid air, they saw that the egg was split right across. Slowly the gap between the two halves widened. They stared.

"*Do* something," moaned Mrs Kane, again. "Quick, Alfred, do something."

"Shush!" said Mr Kane. "Watch!"

And as they watched, a most perfectly beautiful neat, grey little creature parted the stone shell and stepped right out on to the polished tiles of the mantlepiece.

"It's a – it's a – what is it?" whispered Mrs Kane.

"It's a baby kangaroo!" said Mary.

It quite obviously was not, but as nobody else had the least idea what it was, nobody bothered to contradict her. Outside a factory siren began to hoot and they

all jumped. Dan got up and went over to the the mantlepiece.

"Dan!" cried Mrs Kane. "Come away this minute!"

"It's all right, Mum," he said. "It won't bite. Look, you've frightened it now."

The Gift from Winklesea had gone behind the clock. It moved so swiftly that they hardly saw it go. "Look at that!" exclaimed Mr Kane admiringly. "Proper little greyhound!"

He too got up and went over. A small

grey head and beady eye peered from behind the clock face.

"It's looking at us!" cried Mary. "Isn't it sweet!"

"I don't know about sweet," said Mrs Kane. But she, too, came over and joined them. For a few minutes they all stood and looked at the Gift from Winklesea and the Gift from Winklesea looked back at them with a black, unblinking eye.

"Well, then," said Mrs Kane. "What's to be done now?"

"Perhaps it's hungry?" suggested Mary.

"That's it," agreed Mr Kane, grateful for the idea. "Give it a chip, Dan."

Dan fetched one and laid it gently on the shelf a few inches away from the tiny creature. Gradually it came from behind the clock and edged forward.

"It's sniffing!" cried Mary.

It was. Then a mouth of astonishing size suddenly opened and as rapidly closed. The chip had gone.

"Well bless me!" said Mr Kane.

Dan fetched another chip. Then another. Then another. The mouth opened and shut like clockwork.

"No more!" cried Mrs Kane then. "You'll give the poor thing indigestion! It's only a baby, poor thing. Whatever next! Just out of its shell and you feeding it chips as if it was a navvy or something. Give it a saucer of milk, Mary, that's more like what it wants."

A saucer full of milk disappeared in one long, noisy suck.

"There!" cried Mrs Kane triumphantly. "I knew it! Bless its little heart! It was milk he wanted, wasn't it, my lamb?"

The Gift from Winklesea gazed up at her with its black unwinking eyes.

"Now what?" said Mr Kane. The meal seemed to be over.

"Where are we going to put it?" asked Dan.

They all thought.

"There's a mouse cage up in the loft," said Mary.

"No," said Mr Kane. "The aquarium. That's what it wants – a bit of water."

"But you might drown it!" cried Mary.

"No harm in trying," he said. "It came out of the sea, didn't it? You fetch the tank, Dan, from out that cupboard under the sink. Put a bit of water in it and a stone or two, and we'll see what happens."

Half an hour later the Gift from Winklesea was happily swimming in his new home, stopping now and then to gobble the chips that Dan held over the side for him on a fork. Mr Kane was out in the garden digging for worms in case he fancied one of those. Mrs Kane was putting out a note for the milkman to order an extra pint of milk, and Mary just sat and watched, perfectly rapt. The Gift from Winklesea was one of the family now.

Four

The Gift Grows

"It's just that I wish he'd make his mind up," said Mrs Kane next day. She was mopping up wet footprints from the top of the sideboard for what was probably the twentieth time that day. "I wish he'd either go in or stay out."

"He's amphibious," said Dan. "Like a frog."

"Well, this'll have to come off the sideboard," said Mrs Kane. "It'll have to go in the kitchen. Then he can do his paddling about on the tiles, where it's easily mopped up."

So the next time the Gift from Winklesea climbed up on to his rock and came sprawling out on to the polished sideboard his tank was whisked away to a corner of the kitchen. When Mr Kane came home from work he was not too pleased by the arrangement.

"It's not very sociable for the little chap," he objected. "Stuck out there in the kitchen while we're in here. He likes a bit of company, you can see that."

This was certainly true. During his spells on dry land the Gift would go and sit right up close to whoever happened to be in the room. There he would stay with his black, shiny eyes gazing up until he was offered a biscuit or crisp or drink of milk.

"He can come in here once his feet's dry," said Mrs Kane.

And so it was settled. But not for very

long. A day or two later, the next problem cropped up.

"It might be imagination," said Mr Kane, as they sat at supper and the Gift from Winklesea prowled from chair to chair, gobbling up titbits as they were passed down to him, "but I reckon it's four times the size it was when it came out of that egg."

Four pairs of eyes went to the mantelpiece, where the greenish egg, carefully glued back together, still stood on its cockle pedestal. It was at once clear that Mr Kane was right.

"If you ask me," he went on, passing the Gift his third slice of bread and butter, "he doubles up every day."

He watched the eagerly working mouth.

"Do you reckon he's a sea-lion?" he asked.

"No," said Dan. "Not out of an *egg*, Dad."

"I know that," said Mr Kane. "I know

it's not *natural*, coming out of an egg. But he looks a bit like a sea-lion. He's got whiskers coming, look, and a pair of flippers. Though his neck's a bit long, I suppose. Still, could be a *sort* of sea-lion."

"Well he's not stopping in that tank, if he is," said Mrs Kane. "I do draw the line there. You don't think he'll get that size, do you, Father?"

"There's no telling," replied Mr Kane. "That's what *I* think."

"If he's a sea-lion," said Mary, "he ought to be able to catch fish in his mouth, like they do at the zoo."

"We'll try him," said Dan. "Come on."

He held out a piece of seed cake. The Gift watched it unwinkingly.

"Catch!" cried Dan, and tossed the cake.

Quick as lightning it turned, tilted up its head and snap! The cake was gone.

"Good gracious!" cried Mrs Kane.

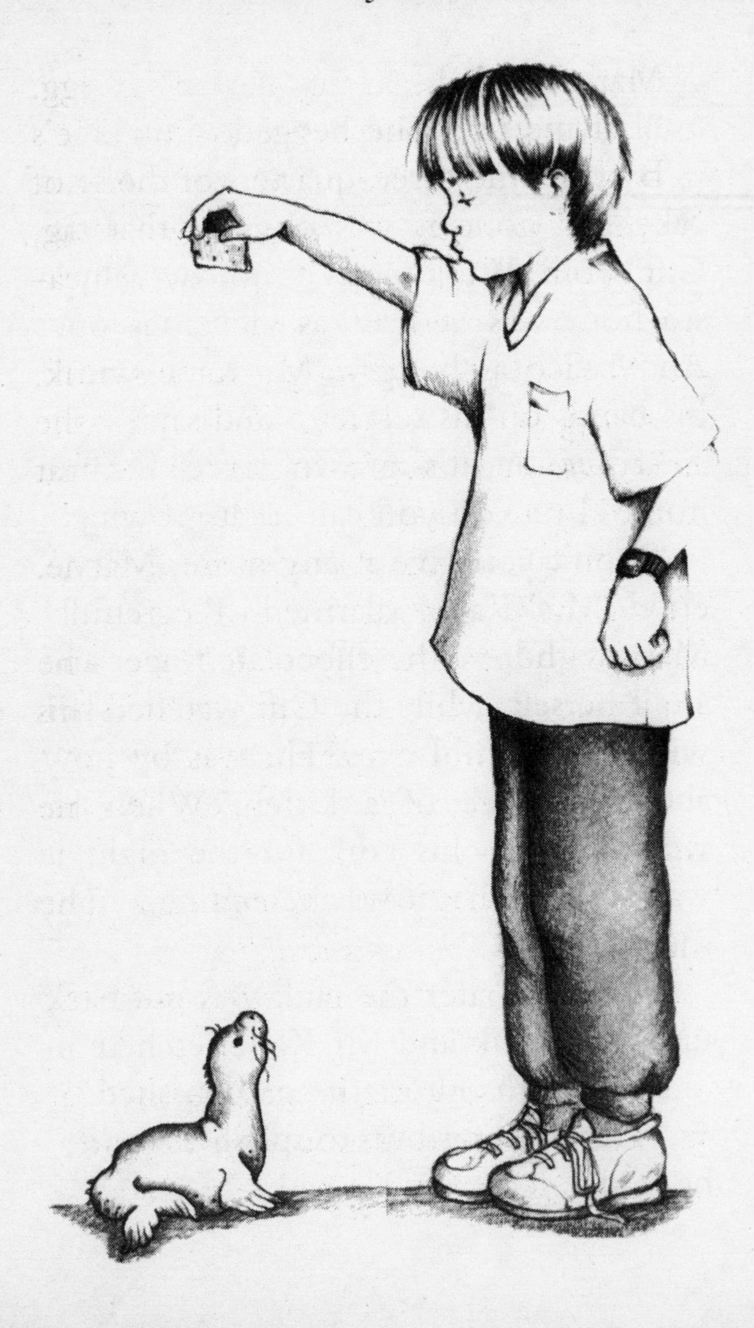

Mary clapped.

"Let me try," she begged.

By the time three-quarters of the seed cake had gone it was obvious that the Gift from Winklesea, if not actually a sea-lion, was at least as clever as one. And twice as hungry. Mr Kane wiped his hands on his serviette and said,

"I reckon it's grown since I came home. I reckon you can *see* it growing."

"Don't you give it any more, Mary," cried Mrs Kane, alarmed. Regretfully Mary withdrew the chocolate finger and ate it herself, while the Gift watched her with reproachful eyes. He was by now about the size of a kitten. When he went back to his tank for the night it was obvious that it was becoming a tight squeeze.

Two days later the tank was put back under the sink and Mr Kane fetched an old zinc bath out of the garden shed.

"This'll do for him to splash about it," he said.

"Not in my kitchen, it won't," said Mrs Kane.

"He can have it out on the lawn," Dan said.

"And we can make a little bed for him in the corner of the kitchen," Mary said. "We can use that old dog basket."

So the Gift from Winklesea, who was now as big as a full grown tabby and as quick on his flippers, was installed in his two new homes – one wet, one dry, according to his mood.

On that day Uncle Fred came round. At the time the Gift was tucking into his pre-supper snack of a bowl of tinned cat food.

"Bless my soul!" said Uncle Fred, staring. "What's that?"

"A sort of sea-lion," said Mary.

"That we don't know, Fred," said Mr Kane. "We're more or less waiting to find out."

"It's a *sea* thing, isn't it?" said Uncle Fred. "What's it doing out of the water?"

"It's ambidextrous," explained Mr Kane.

"Amphibious," said Dan. "He's got a bath out in the garden when he feels like a swim."

"Rum sort of pet," said Uncle Fred. "Where's it from?"

"There," said Mrs Kane. She pointed. Uncle Fred's eyes followed her finger. His gaze fell on the egg with the dark, unmistakable crack running from top to bottom. His jaw dropped.

"You don't mean to say—?"

"Yes, Fred," nodded Mr Kane. "We *do*."

Uncle Fred's eyes went from the egg to the rug and then back to the egg.

"Well I'm blessed!" he said at last. "That great big thing down there came out of that little egg up there?"

"That's about the size of it," agreed Mr Kane.

The Gift from Winklesea, his bowl empty, came sniffing eagerly towards

Uncle Fred. Hastily he tucked his legs under his chair.

"Don't bite, does he?" he said.

"Not that we know of," said Mr Kane comfortingly. "Do you, old chap?" He reached down and patted the sleek grey back. Uncle Fred watched.

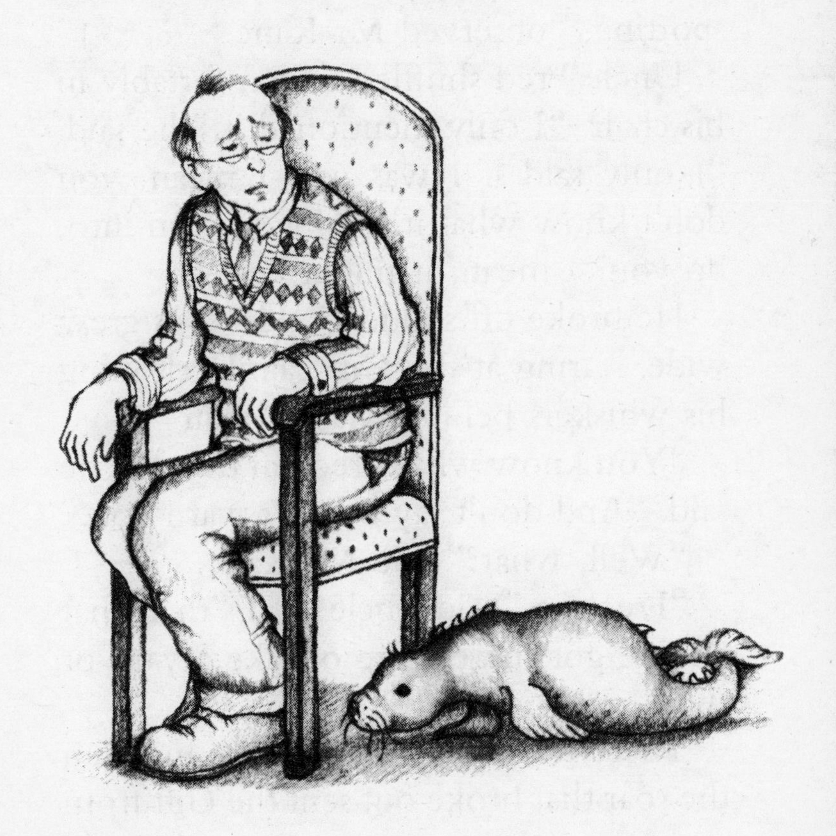

"If I was you," he said, "I should get that put away in a zoo."

The Kanes turned on him.

"In a zoo!" exclaimed Dan.

"But he's a pet!" cried Mary.

"I'm surprised at you, Fred," said Mrs Kane severely, and "*That's* not very sporting," observed Mr Kane.

Uncle Fred shuffled uncomfortably in his chair. "I only mentioned it," he said. "I only said if I was *you*. I mean, you don't know what it's going to turn into, do you? I mean, it might be—"

He broke off suddenly. His eyes grew wide, staring at the Gift calmly cleaning his whiskers behind Mary's chair.

"You know what I reckon that is?" he said. "And don't say I didn't warn you."

"Well, what?" said Mr Kane.

"I reckon," said Uncle Fred, "that what you've got there, give or take a yard or two – is a Loch Ness Monster!"

There was a moment's silence and then the roar that broke out sent the Gift from

Winklesea in one smooth graceful slither to the back of the television set where he lay trembling till the laughter finally died away.

"Oh dear," said Mr Kane, wiping his eyes, "you are a comic, Fred. Come and give me a hand with the hose."

"What for?" he asked, getting up and following him out.

"Water the tomatoes. And fill the bath up for the Loch Ness Monster!"

His laughter came floating back over his shoulders and the Gift from Winklesea, Mary was quite certain, widened his mouth into something that was very like his first smile.

Winklesea. [illegible] to the back of [illegible] where he [illegible] all the laughter finally died away.

'Oh dear,' said Mr Kane, wiping his eyes. 'You are a comic, Fred. Come and give me a hand with the hose.'

'What for?' he asked, getting up and following him out.

'Water the tomatoes. And fill the bath up for the Loch Ness Monster.'

His laughter came floating back over his shoulders, and the calf from Winklesea, Mary was quite certain, widened its mouth into something that was very like its first smile.

Five

A Fish out of Water

Whenever Mary looked back on these days afterwards, she decided that the middle period was the best, the days when the Gift was about the size of a lamb – and twice as frisky. The whole family doted on him, and he would lie in the evenings alongside Mrs Kane's chair while she did her knitting, gazing up at her. She was very pleased and flattered by this attention, though she tried hard not to show it, and declared that he was "just like Rosy" (a dachshund she had once had) and "ever so affectionate, for all his tricks".

Mary and Dan thought that his soulful gaze was an expression more of hunger than affection, but did not like to spoil things for their mother by saying so. Besides, this habit helped Mrs Kane to overlook the "little tricks", which included nipping into the kitchen and snapping up any food that he found in sight, and bowling a metal bucket noisily up and down the yard for hours on end.

"Clatter bang clatter from morning to night," she would say. "It's really getting on my nerves."

"He'll grow out of it," observed Mr Kane. "Like a baby's rattle for him, as you might say."

"He's probably trying to tell us he's hungry," Mary said. "That's the pail we fetch the scraps in."

"And that's another thing," Mrs Kane said. "Hungry! It's enough to make you wonder if there's not something the matter with him. He probably needs some injections, or something, like dogs have."

"It's natural at his age," Mr Kane said. "I can remember when I was a boy, three helpings at every meals and bread and jam in between, and—"

"Don't you go comparing him with *you*," interrupted Mrs Kane. "*You* didn't gobble up eight pails of scraps a day, I should hope. There's a bit of difference between eight pails of scraps and a few slices of bread and jam."

At this point Mr Kane had sucked noisily at his pipe and begun the lengthy process of relighting it.

At any rate, they all still looked on the Gift from Winklesea as a pet – however unusual – and put up with his inconvenient little ways with as good a grace as possible.

Then came the affair of the church bazaar, and the whole question as to whether in fact the Gift was a pet at all was raised, with a good deal of heart searching for everyone, from the Vicar downwards. It began the day Dan came back from an errand waving a printed sheet of paper.

"Listen to this!" he cried. The rest of the family, impressed, listened. "'Children's Pet Show – dozens of prizes to be won. Bring along your pet for the judging, 11 a.m. prompt, by Mr Jake Hunter of the Corner Pet Shop.'"

"That the church bazaar, then?" inquired Mr Kane. "They're making a big do of it this year. Got to. That organ's got to be mended, or the Vicar'll lose half his customers. Puts a blight over the whole service, and an insult to a good hymn tune."

Mr Kane was a member of the church choir and felt very strongly about the organ.

"Pet Show, is there?" said Mrs Kane. "Well I hope there won't be too much straw and mess and that in the church hall." Mrs Kane was a volunteer scrubber-out.

"Dan!" Mary could see what he was driving at, even if the others couldn't. "You mean we can enter the Gift!"

"Of course. He's a pet, isn't he? He'll walk it. Here you are, Winkie!"

He tossed a handful of biscuits through the open window and the Gift caught most of them in flight.

"What else does it say?" asked Mary.

"It says, 'Entry forms and further details available from the Corner Pet Shop or from the Vicar'," said Dan. "Hang on, I'll be back."

After supper that night the table was cleared and the Kanes pored over the entry form and further details of the Children's Pet Show.

" 'All animals must be housed in a suitable container provided by the entrant'," Dan read out. " 'All entries to be brought to the church hall by 10 a.m. ready for the judging at 11 a.m.' "

"Suitable container, eh?" said Mr Kane thoughtfully. "*That's* a stickler."

"We'll have to get a really big crate," said Dan, "and then put some wire netting across."

"Oh Dan!" cried Mary. "He'll hate it!"

"He won't be in there for long," Dan said. "Pity is that he can't be in a bath, or something. He'd show up far better in water."

The Kanes discussed this for a while but in the end decided that a bath would probably not come under the heading of a "suitable container".

"I'll fix up a crate at work," said Mr Kane, "and drop it off at the church hall Friday night. I shall be round there anyhow, putting up stalls."

"And how will we get the Gift there?" asked Dan. "You'll need the car Saturday morning, won't you, Dad?"

Mr Kane nodded.

"The wheelbarrow!" cried Mary. "We can take him in the wheelbarrow! He loves that."

This was true. One of the Gift's favourite games was being trundled round the garden at a breakneck pace and ending by being tipped unceremoniously into his bath.

"I don't know what people will think

about *that,*" ventured Mrs Kane.

"Susan Platt took her hedgehog to school in a wheelbarrow," said Mary.

"And Jim Carter used to bring his kid brother down to the park in one," said Dan.

Mrs Kane was overruled.

" 'Animals will be judged on the usual points, including general condition and good grooming'," said Mr Kane.

"We'll give him a good scrub," said Dan.

"And brush him," said Mary. "Could we tie a ribbon round his neck, or something?"

"No, we couldn't," said Dan.

"*That* one don't need no trimmings," observed Mr Kane. "In the pink, he is. Any judge can see that. Now, what's this? 'Animals will be judged in the following classes: Dogs, Cats, Mice and Hamsters, Rabbits, Birds.' "

The Kanes looked at each other.

"Which of them d'ye reckon he is, then?" said Mr Kane at last.

"None of them," said Mary.

"He's got to be entered as one of 'em," pointed out Mr Kane. "Dog is about the nearest, wouldn't you say, Mother?"

"Dog!" cried Dan.

"Well, nearest in size," said Mr Kane. "And that yapping he does . . ." His voice trailed off.

Dan took the printed form and read it again.

"Here, what's this!" he cried. "Look – at the bottom. 'There will also be a special class for tropical fish and other aquarium pets.' That's it!"

"Tropical *fish*?" echoed Mr Kane. "*Him*?"

"It says 'other aquarium pets'," said Dan. "And the Gift used to be in one – before he outgrew it, that is. He'll definitely have to go in that class, Dad.

Anyone can see he's not a dog or a cat or a rabbit or anything."

And so the form was carefully filled in with the Gift vaguely described as "Aquarium Pet", and Dan went off with it to the Vicarage.

"Seems rum to me," remarked Mr Kane when he had gone. "It'll be the first time *that* chap's had to judge a fish out of water, I'll be bound. But perhaps he'll come round to the idea when we explain."

That was what they all hoped.

Six

Aquarium Pet

Next morning Dan and Mary spent a full hour grooming the Gift from Winklesea.

"Not that there's much need to bother," Dan said. "He'll win hands down."

"He does shine, though, now he's had a good shampoo and brush," said Mary. She had enjoyed the whole performance and the Gift was very obliging about it all. He did a good deal of splashing, of course, but as Dan and Mary were wearing swimsuits, that only added to the fun. And now he really did look beautiful, his sleek grey coat shining in the sunlight, his long neck rearing up so proudly that Mary almost brought up the subject of a ribbon again.

Dan scrubbed out the wheelbarrow, Mary filled a carrier bag with biscuits for the Gift's elevenses, and they were ready.

"He really does look a picture," agreed Mrs Kane, when called upon for her verdict. "Though I still can't help wondering what people are going to think about *that* going up the road in a wheelbarrow."

They set off, the Gift sitting bolt upright in his chariot, blinking about him with interest and cringing only ever so slightly as cars and motor cycles sped by. Dan pushed and Mary kept close by him, feeling that the Gift really did seem like a proper pet now that they were taking him for an airing, if not an actual walk. She wondered whether they could buy him a collar and lead with the money he won for his prize, and then he could go for real walks.

Things were quiet until they reached the main road. Even then all would have been well if Dan had not had to run across the road. The increased speed, the rattling of the wheels and the sudden jolt as the wheelbarrow went over the kerb, excited the Gift. He evidently thought that the usual game was about to start, and once at the other side of the road stood right up and began whooping, throwing back his head and beating his chest and rocking the wheelbarrow to a dangerous tilt.

"Sit *down*!" hissed Dan. Passers-by halted in their tracks. People began to appear from nowhere. "Sit down!"

Fatally, he hastened his pace. The Gift was beside himself with delight.

"Be careful!" Mary cried. "Oh Dan, look out! If he falls out he'll get all dirty again!"

Dan let the handles of the wheelbarrow fall so abruptly that the Gift nearly fell out anyway.

"We'll stop a minute and let him calm down," he said.

The Gift sat and looked about him at his audience. There were about fifteen or twenty people, including a policeman. "What's all this about, then?" he demanded. His eyes fell on the Gift. "What – what – what . . . ?"

"We're just taking him down to the church hall for the pet show and we'll have to be going now or we'll be late," said Dan rapidly, and picked up the handles of the wheelbarrow.

"Just a minute," said the Law. "Is that a *wild* animal? Or a domestic?"

"He's a – he's a domestic wild animal," said Dan.

"Because if it's domestic it'll want a licence, and if it's wild it ought to be in a cage. Name and address?"

Dan gave them. The crowd increased.

When Dan set off again quite a lot of them followed. They all kept saying. "What is it? What is it?" and Dan replied firmly. "An aquarium pet."

By the time they reached the church hall he had said this so many times that he had come to believe it himself, so that when the Vicar, meeting him at the porch, asked the same question, he answered without hesitation.

"My word," said the Vicar. "How very strange. We learn something new about the created world every day, do we not?"

"Yes, Mr Gibbon," said Dan.

The pet show was staged at the far end of the hall. They left the wheelbarrow outside and the Gift bounded happily along with them and unsuspectingly followed a trail of biscuits into his crate. Dan whipped across the wire netting and next minute the Gift was caged. He looked altogether different behind the mesh. Dan and Mary stared at him and as soon as the last biscuit had been downed he stared back.

"Oh, Dan," said Mary. "I can't *bear* him being in a cage."

"It's not for long," Dan said. He couldn't, either. The Gift was their friend and now, caged, he was no longer their equal. The Gift himself did not seem to be taking it so hard as Dan and Mary themselves. He was giving little excited leaps and staring feverishly at something beyond them.

There, lined up in tanks, were his fellow competitors. Beautiful, vacant, dreamy fish went winding among their weeds and shells. The Gift began to whimper and scrabble at the wire netting.

"Oh Dan!" cried Mary. "It must remind him of home. It reminds him of the sea!"

"More likely wants to eat them," Dan said. Mary, alarmed, lifted a corner of the netting and dropped in a handful of biscuits.

Three boys halted by the crate.

"What's that?" asked one.

"Aquarium Pet," said Dan.

"It's not! It never! Hear that, Pete? That's not an aquarium pet!"

"It is!" said Mary hotly. "I mean, *he* is!"

"Where's its aquarium, then?" demanded Pete.

"He's outgrown it," said Dan. "He uses a bath now, instead. But we couldn't bring that."

"Look! There's Mr Hunter just come in with the Vicar. Let's ask him!"

They raced off. Dan and Mary looked at each other and then at the Gift from Winklesea, still intent on the tropical fish.

"I'm not letting him be beaten by a fish!" said Dan fiercely, as the group approached him, talking excitedly.

"Great heaven!" exclaimed Mr Hunter when he saw the Gift. "You say this lives in an aquarium?"

"He would if we had one big enough," Dan said. "He outgrew the fish tank."

"He's not a fish, though, is he, sir?" cried one of the boys eagerly.

"Not strictly," said Mr Hunter. "He's evidently amphibious."

"Well it's not fair him being put in with my fish," said Pete.

"Oh stop it!" cried Mary. "Let's take him home, Dan. Come on."

She could hardly wait to have the Gift back where he belonged, lording it over the back garden from his bath tub and banqueting merrily from morning till night. She pulled at the wire netting.

"One moment, one moment," said the Vicar. "If I could just have a word with you, Mr Hunter?"

They retired a little way off and talked in low voices while the two parties glowered at each other. Then the Vicar came over, beaming.

"All is well,' he said. "Mr Hunter has agreed that there should be a special prize offered for 'The most unusual pet'. We shan't of course know for certain until after eleven o'clock," he coughed, "but I think it likely – extremely likely, that your pet will be judged outstanding in that category." He took another long

look at the Gift over his spectacles. "He *is* unusual," he said, and went to inspect the haberdashery stall.

The Gift was not only judged the most unusual pet, receiving a prize of fifty pence and a blue rosette. He also "practically did up the organ single-handed," as Mr Kane told everyone afterwards. Throughout the day as his fame spread, so did the crowds. A special queue had to be organized from the door to his crate. He stayed till teatime, basking in his glory and bringing the Vicar more tenpenny pieces than he had imagined in his wildest dreams. Fifty people followed his triumphal ride home in the wheelbarrow.

The Kanes had a fish and chip supper to celebrate, with a double portion for the Gift.

"Every dog has his day," remarked Mr Kane, spearing a forkful of plaice. "And *he*," with a jerk of the fork, "has had his, I reckon."

There was a loud snore from somewhere under the table. The Gift from Winklesea had had too much excitement and eaten too many chips. His day was certainly over.

Seven
Trouble

By the end of the second week the Gift from Winklesea was about the size of a sheep and Mrs Kane was beginning to worry about what the neighbours were saying.

"It's that Mrs Baines that's the worst," she said. "'What is it? What is it?' she says, every time I see her."

"And what do you tell her, Mum?" asked Dan.

"I tell her he's a sea-lion," said his mother.

"Oh Mum!" cried Mary. "Anyone can see he's not that!"

"I say he's a *rare* kind of sea-lion," said Mrs Kane. "And for all we know, so he is."

"At the rate he's growing he'll more likely be a rare kind of sea *elephant*," said Dan.

They sat silent. Outside in the garden they could hear vigorous splashing and the curious, high, yapping noises that meant the Gift was enjoying himself.

"That means the hose on again," observed Mrs Kane. "He's only got to *sit* in the bath these days to empty it."

"I'll do it, Mum." Dan went out. Mary followed. They both stared out through the kitchen window to where the Gift, his bath over, was strolling about the garden, drying off. As he walked his long neck had a curious nodding movement, like that of a gander.

"I wish he'd stop growing," said Mary. It was not that she herself liked him any the less for being big, just that she could see that their mother *did*.

"You know," Dan said, turning on the tap, "Uncle Fred was right. He does look a bit like the Loch Ness Monster."

He and Mary had found a book about it in the school library. It had showed all kinds of pre-historic monsters, too, and none of them looked entirely unlike the Gift.

"I heard Mum tell Dad last night that if he grew much more we'd have to take him back to the shop," said Mary.

"A bull in a china shop!" said Dan. He began to laugh at his own joke. Mary couldn't even see that it was a joke.

"D'you think she'd give us our forty pence back?" said Dan, and was off again.

"*You* might think you're funny," said Mary, and went out into the garden.

The Gift from Winklesea nodded and waddled his way towards her. His nose, as always, was twitching. Mary took the biscuit from her pocket. All her pocket-money nowadays seemed to go on biscuits. She bought the broken ones from the supermarket, at half price.

"I wish you wouldn't eat so much," Mary told him now. He regarded her with his boot button eyes. She felt quite sure that he knew what she was saying. Mr Kane said he was very intelligent and could be trained. Mrs Kane had wanted to know "Trained for what?" but he hadn't been sure about that.

"Just simple commands," he had said at last. "You know – Sit, and Stay and Beg."

Dan was interested in the idea. He had already got the Gift coming to a special whistle. He was intelligent, all right.

The Gift, realizing that there were no more biscuits, looked wistfully at his bath, slowly filling with water from the hose, then went and sat in the shade of the hollyhocks. It was a very hot day. He was panting, and moved slowly.

I hope he's not going to be ill, thought Mary, alarmed. She wondered what the PDSA vet would make of the Gift if they had to take him there. When her father came home, she said.

"Dad, after tea, could we let the Gift go for a swim in the canal? We've filled his bath about ten times today, but the minute he gets in it's empty after one good splash."

"Good idea," said Mr Kane. "He'll enjoy that."

So after tea they unlocked the gate at the bottom of the garden and in two bounds the Gift from Winklesea was over the tow-path and in the water. The Kanes were showered with spray. He ducked and dived and threshed and paddled, throwing back his long neck and letting out high whoops of excitement.

"Fetch the camera, Dan," said Mr Kane, wiping down his suit with his handkerchief. "Let's get a picture of him."

Mrs Baker next door came down to the bottom of her garden and watched over the fence.

"Well I never! He ought to be in a circus!"

The Gift was showing off now, turning somersaults and doing nose dives with his tail left standing up clear out of the water.

"There's a pail of scraps by the back door if you want to fetch it, Mary," she said. Mary followed her. Most of the neighbours were saving their scraps for the Gift now. He didn't turn up his nose at anything. Potato peelings, apple rinds, stale bread, old cheese – it all flowed steadily into wide, busy jaws.

Back on the tow-path Mary found the others busy taking pictures of the Gift. He leaped and twirled obligingly.

"Proper film star," said Mr Kane admiringly. "Pity we haven't got ciné."

"I'll go and put his scraps out," said Mary.

Next minute a wet grey shape bowled past her. It was the Gift. He had only to hear the rattle of a pail or chink of cutlery, and he was there, instantaneously, nose twitching, black eyes greedy. The Kanes went in and left him with his nose buried in the pail.

"Had a good splash, did he?" asked Mrs Kane. "I could see the spray from here."

"He loved it," Mary said. For a moment she felt guilty. The Gift was from the sea – he was meant to live in the sea. All he had here was a zinc bath and sometimes a splash in the canal as a treat. She pictured him riding waves, vaulting breakers, and wondered if he were really happy.

"You'd better all come in the other room," said Mrs Kane. "We've all got to have a good talk about everything."

Mary and Dan made faces at each other and followed her in.

"It's just that we've got to be sensible," began Mrs Kane. "Nothing like this has ever happened to us before, and it's hard to know what to do for the best."

Mary stared at her.

"You're not going to say he's got to go!" she blurted.

"I don't really see how we're to keep him, dear. He's eating us out of house and home, and look at the size of him, I mean, we don't know when he's going to *stop*."

"I thought you liked him," Mary said.

"I do. At least, I did when he first came out of there." She waved her hand towards the stone egg. "I just didn't bargain for him turning out like this."

"You can't give him away," said Dan quickly. "He's a present. You can't give presents away."

"But I've still got the real present. It's lovely up there on the mantelpiece. I shall still have that."

"No,' said Dan. "The Gift's the real present. Isn't he, Mary?"

She nodded. In the silence that followed the Kanes were suddenly aware of a commotion in the garden. Unmistakably came the high, indignant yapping that meant the Gift had been thwarted. It was the noise had made when you showed him a pound of biscuits and only gave him half a dozen.

As they reached the back door the Gift was re-entering the garden. Behind him came Mrs Baker, yard brush raised aloft, her own shrieks mingling horribly with those of the Gift. With a final flourish of the brush she slammed the gate shut and stood triumphant on the other side, panting mightily, face crimson.

"And don't you come back!" she shouted. "Thieving little monster! And don't you come round here begging for my scraps again!"

The Gift from Winklesea went behind the dustbin. The Kanes advanced cautiously and Mrs Baker caught sight of them.

"Would you believe it!" she cried. "He's only just this minute had a great bucket full of scraps, and now he's after my cabbages. Ate half a row he had, before I spotted him. And what Mr Baker'll have to say when he gets back I daren't hardly think."

Mr Kane made all the apologies.

"I can't think how that gate got left open," he said. "It won't happen again, I'll see to that."

The Gift crept out from his hiding-place and Mrs Baker's baleful eye again lighted on him.

"That animal," she said, "has growed since yesterday, I swear it. I was only saying to Mr Baker last night, that animal'd eat anything. It's not natural. What you've got to be careful of," she paused dramatically, "is that he don't start going round eating *humans*!"

The words out, she gave a sudden shriek at the very thought of it, clapped a hand over her mouth and was gone. The Kanes watched the yard brush go rapidly along the top of the hedge and disappear. For a time no one spoke.

"Bad boy," said Mrs Kane to the Gift from Winklesea. "*Bad* boy." He looked at her, his eyes woeful.

"Well just make sure that gate isn't left open again," she said. "It's putting temptation in his way, and it's not fair. You know what he's like for his food."

They did. Mr Kane looked at his watch.

"It's supper time now," he said. "get his bowl, Dan."

It was feeding time again.

Eight

The Gift Decides

In the next week the canal gate was kept firmly shut, there were no more complaints from the neighbours, and the Gift from Winklesea grew at least another yard in all directions. He was now the size of a donkey, and any idea of his being a kind of sea-lion, however, rare, had been finally abandoned. Even Mr Kane, who at first had enjoyed seeing the Gift "double up" daily, was becoming gloomy.

"It's not natural," he would say, staring out to where the Gift would sit gazing wistfully through the gate at the canal. "Even *elephants* don't grow that quick. Takes them years to get that size. *Years.*"

Uncle Fred, who had become a frequent caller, was all for taking the Gift down to the PDSA and handing him in.

"They'll see to him," he said, "it's their job. It's what they're there for."

"But he's not a *stray*, Fred," objected Mr Kane.

"In a manner of speaking he is," said Uncle Fred. "Strayed from the sea, you might say. They could pop him in one of their vans and get him back down there quick as a wink. Quick as a Winklesea."

He guffawed. The Kanes watched him with unsmiling faces. Rapidly he straightened his own.

"All I'm saying is," he said, "that you've got to get him out of here before he gets to his full size."

"And what size do you reckon that'll be Fred?" inquired Mr Kane.

"I told you," said Uncle Fred. "A Loch Ness Monster, that's what he is. He'll be curled up three times round the garden before you've finished if you don't move fast."

Mrs Kane let out a squeal.

"Oh go on with you, Fred!" she said nervously.

"I mean it," said Uncle Fred, and left.

When he had gone Mr Kane said, "He could be right, you know."

"Right about what, Dad?" asked Dan.

"About the PDSA."

"Oh *Dad*!" cried Mary.

"It'd be kindest, in the long run," he went on. "I mean, if they was to take him back where he belongs. Look at him now, peering over the gate at the canal with eyes like organ stops. *Pining* for a bit of water, he is."

This time Mary said nothing. It was

true. Even Dan, who enjoyed an argument, was silent.

"We'll take him tomorrow, then, shall we?" said Mr Kane at last. No one said anything. Mary got up and stood with her face pressed against the window, staring at the blurred grey shape of the patient Gift. It seemed such a shabby way for it all to end – to get *rid* of him, as if he were some kind of pest, instead of the most magical and delightful thing that had ever happened to them.

As it happened, the PDSA never had to decide whether or not the Gift was a genuine stray – he took things into his own hands.

Next day Mary, running as usual to her bedroom window to toss down his early morning biscuits into the Gift's eager jaws, saw that he had gone. Even at a glance she saw it – for there was nothing in the garden big enough to hide him.

All the same she threw open the window.

"Winkie! Winkie!" she cried.

The night before she had lain awake longing for a miracle. But now that the garden was empty, the sun shafting up from the cucumber frames half blinding her, it did not seem like a miracle at all.

The Kanes gathered in the garden, looking for clues. The wicket gate was still firmly shut.

"He's jumped over," said Mr Kane. "We ought to've known he'd do that, sooner or later."

"Almost as if he'd known," said Mrs Kane tearfully. "I don't know how we could even've *dreamed* of getting rid of him. Poor little orphan."

"Not exactly an orphan," said Mr Kane.

"Well he came out of an egg," she said, "and an *egg* isn't much of a family."

"It could be all for the best," said Mr Kane. "After all, he's back in the water now, where he belongs. Likely as not he'll find his way back to the sea now."

They went back in to have their breakfast. The day seemed long and empty without the Gift.

"It's the mealtimes you miss more than anything," said Mrs Kane at supper. "There was never a dull minute with him to feed."

Mr Kane appeared suddenly from behind his evening paper with a shout that made the rest jump.

"Here! What about this!"

He pointed to a heavy black headline.

CANAL MYSTERY –
BARGEMAN TELLS OF STRANGE
MONSTER

"Would you believe it!" cried Mrs Kane.

"He's *not* a monster!" cried Mary.

"What happened?" asked Dan.

Mr Kane read out the story. It turned out that a certain Bill Barr, who was taking his narrow boat down to a nearby town, had suddenly turned to see a "grey, long-necked monster" snapping up his sandwiches that lay on the deck behind him.

"That's the Gift all right!" cried Dan jubilantly. "Good old Winkie!"

Mr Barr had not been able to say anything else about the monster because he had then fallen into the canal and by the time he climbed out the creature was gone. He was now in hospital suffering from shock and had told reporters that it was the last time that he would ever go on that run. All he could say was that the monster had had "great snapping jaws" and was roughly the size of an elephant but with a giraffe's neck.

"What a fib!" cried Mary. "It's nothing like him!"

"It *is* him, though," Dan said. "Beating up the canals like anything. Near Witham, it says. That's half-way to Winklesea."

They stared at each other in sudden glee. The Gift had solved his own problem. He had taken leave of his own accord, as a guest should. He was following his own nose back to the sea where he belonged, *splashing* his way home, up the canals.

"He'll miss his biscuits," said Mr Kane, when it had all sunk in. "Loved his biscuits, he did."

"We could always go down there one week-end," said Mrs Kane. "And you give him a whistle, Dan."

"Oh *yes*!" cried Mary.

"*That*'d soon clear the beach," remarked Mr Kane.

"We shall have to start saving up for biscuits," Dan said. "How much did we have left after the outing?"

"Well there is one thing," Mrs Kane said. "We've still got his egg."

They all looked at it, looking just like any other seaside souvenir but for the unmistakable brown crack running the length of the blue-green stone.

"It was worth forty pence," Mary said. "All that for forty pence."

"And I've just thought of something else," Dan said.

They all looked at him.

"That shop might have some more the same. Get your pig, Mary, and let's count up. We could have two this time, maybe *three*!"

"No!" said Mrs Kane.

But Dan and Mary exchanged triumphant glances. It was Dan's birthday this month, and Mary had to give him something. She *had* thought of a magnifying glass, but a Gift from Winklesea suddenly seemed a much better idea. *Very* much better . . .

Mystery at Winklesea

Helen Cresswell

The magical Gift from Winklesea hatched from an egg bought by Dan and Mary, and changed their lives forever. He lives by the sea for most of the year, but now he's coming home to spend the winter with his friends. But he's homesick, and causing havoc with the neighbours.

Why does he have that mournful look on his face? And *how* does he manage to be in two places at once? The mystery deepens. Perhaps there's more to the Gift than meets the eye . . .

ORDER FORM

0 340 64648 9	WHATEVER HAPPENED IN WINKLESEA? *Helen Cresswell (hardback)*	£8.99	☐
0 340 64643 8	MYSTERY AT WINKLESEA *Helen Cresswell (paperback)*	£3.50	☐

All Hodder Children's books are available at your local bookshop or newsagent, or can be ordered direct from the publisher. Just tick the titles you want and fill in the form below. Prices and availability subject to change without notice.

Hodder Children's Books, Cash Sales Department, Bookpoint, 39 Milton Park, Abingdon, OXON, OX14 4TD, UK. If you have a credit card you may order by telephone – (01235) 831700.

Please enclose a cheque or postal order made payable to Bookpoint Ltd to the value of the cover price and allow the following for postage and packing: UK & BFPO – £1.00 for the first book, 50p for the second book and 30p for each additional book ordered up to a maximum charge of £3.00.
OVERSEAS & EIRE – £2.00 for the first book, £1.00 for the second book and 50p for each additional book.

Name ....

Address ....

....

....

If you would prefer to pay by credit card, please complete:
Please debit my Visa/Access/Diner's Card/American Express (delete as applicable) card no:

Signature ....

Expiry Date ....